A MESSAGE TO PARENTS

Reading good books to young children is a crucial factor in a child's psychological and intellectual development. It promotes a mutually warm and satisfying relationship between parent and child and enhances the child's awareness of the world around him. It stimulates the child's imagination and lays a foundation for the development of the skills necessary to support the critical thinking process. In addition, the parent who reads to his child helps him to build vocabulary and other prerequisite skills for the child's own successful reading.

In order to provide parents and children with books which will do these things, Brown Watson has published this series of small books specially designed for young children. These books are factual, fanciful, humorous, questioning and adventurous. A library acquired in this inexpensive way will provide many hours of pleasurable and profitable reading for parents and children.

Ten
Little
MONKEYS

By JESSICA
POTTER
BRODERICK

Illustrated by
KATHERINE
L. PHILLIPS

Cover illustration by Irma Wilde

Brown Watson

England

In a jungle,

    far away,

Tiny monkeys

    romp and play.

1

Through banyan branches,
just for fun,
Hunt for monkeys.
You'll find *one*.

ONE

2

High up,

    playing peek-a-boo

Around a palm tree,

    you'll find *two*.

TWO

3

Swinging on vines

from tree to tree,

Find and count them,

one, two, *three*.

THREE

4

See them! There are

more and more!

Playing leapfrog

you'll find *four*.

FOUR

5

Splashing in

a running brook,

You'll find *five*,

if you just look.

FIVE

6

They have fun

with stones and sticks.

If you hunt,

you will find *six*.

SIX

7

Picking flowers

and eating fruit,

There are *seven*.

Aren't they cute?

SEVEN

8

Near tall trees

and grassy huts,

Eight play ball

with coconuts.

EIGHT

9

Skippity-hopping

in a line,

And somersaulting,

you'll find *nine*.

NINE

10

Dancing gaily

round and round,

Ten little monkeys

can be found.

TEN

You've found them

every one, and then,

You've also learned

to count to ten!

TEN